The adventures of Monty

Monty Falls in Love

AUTHOR

Jessie Wee has had 12 years of teaching experience, both in Primary and Secondary schools. Since giving up teaching, she has been writing children's stories, over a 100 of which have appeared in children's magazines. THE ADVENTURES OF MONTY is her first collection of stories to be published in book form.

Story by Jessie Wee
Pictures by Kwan Shan Mei

ILLUSTRATOR

Kwan Shan Mei, a gifted artist, has set a very high standard for herself in the illustrations she does for children's books. This Shanghai-educated artist has done a short period of understudy with the great master Chow Han Mei. She has developed a varied style and always strives to bring out .... in each of

FEDERAL PUBLICATIONS
Singapore • Kuala Lumpur • Hong Kong

© 1987 Federal Publications (S) Pte Ltd
Times Jurong
2 Jurong Port Road
Singapore 2261

First published 1987

ISBN 9971 4 1432 5

Printed in Singapore by Koon Wah Printing Pte Ltd

for my sons
ANDY and DEREK

One day, Monty decided to visit his old home.
He waved goodbye to all his friends.

He crossed the green field and walked and walked
until he came to Grandma's house.

Monty crept into the sitting room.
Everything was quiet.
He crept into the kitchen.
There was no one there.

Monty went into his little hole.
There were cobwebs all over the place.

The house was empty.
Grandma had moved away.

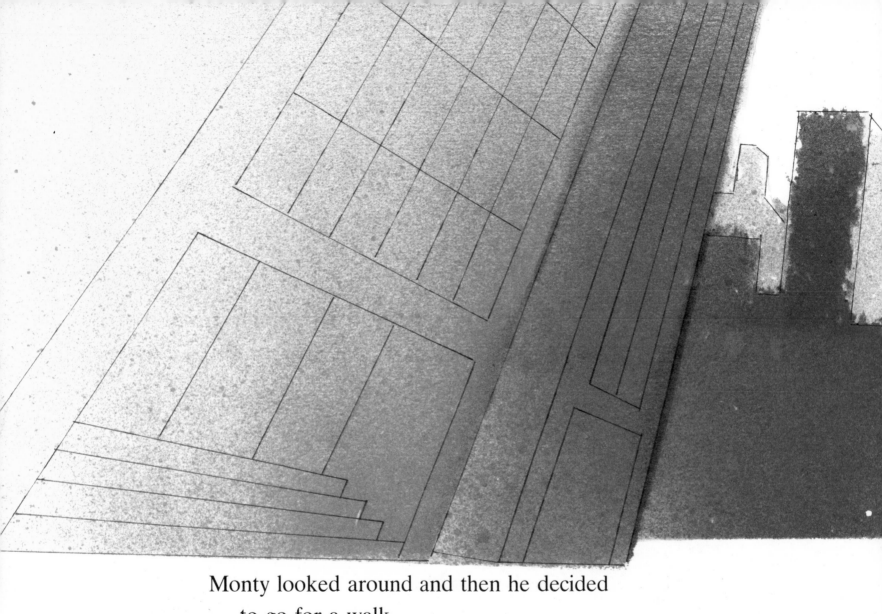

Monty looked around and then he decided
  to go for a walk.
He walked across the road.
He walked around the town.
He looked at the shops.

He looked at the blocks of ten-story buildings.
He looked at the fountain in the shopping complex.
He liked everything he saw.

Soon, it was time to go home.
Monty walked up and down the streets.
He walked round and round the town.
He crossed the road, but he could not
    find his way home.

Poor Monty! He was lost!

Sad and frightened, he crept
under a bridge to hide.

And there, he met the prettiest little mouse he had ever
    set eyes on.
She had a pink nose and a long, curly tail.
She was as white as the clouds on a bright, sunny day.

"Hello!" she said. "I'm Candy. Who are you?"

"I'm Monty and I'm lost."

"I'll help you," said Candy.

"I'll show you the way home."

Monty was no longer sad.
He was no longer afraid.
Candy, his new friend,
would show him the way home.

They walked and they walked
   until they came to the green field.
Monty was home!

All the animals came to meet Monty.
They all liked Candy.

They thought her the prettiest little mouse
they had ever set eyes on.
Everyone asked Candy to stay.

Mother Bird found her a little house not far from the pond.

Monty was very happy.
He was glad Candy had come to stay.
He liked Candy very, very much.
Candy liked him too.

One day, when the skies were blue and the
flowers were blooming in the green field,
Monty told Candy how much he loved her.

Candy loved Monty too, so they were married in a little
    church by the pond.
Candy looked beautiful and Monty looked so handsome.
They made a lovely pair as they walked down the aisle.

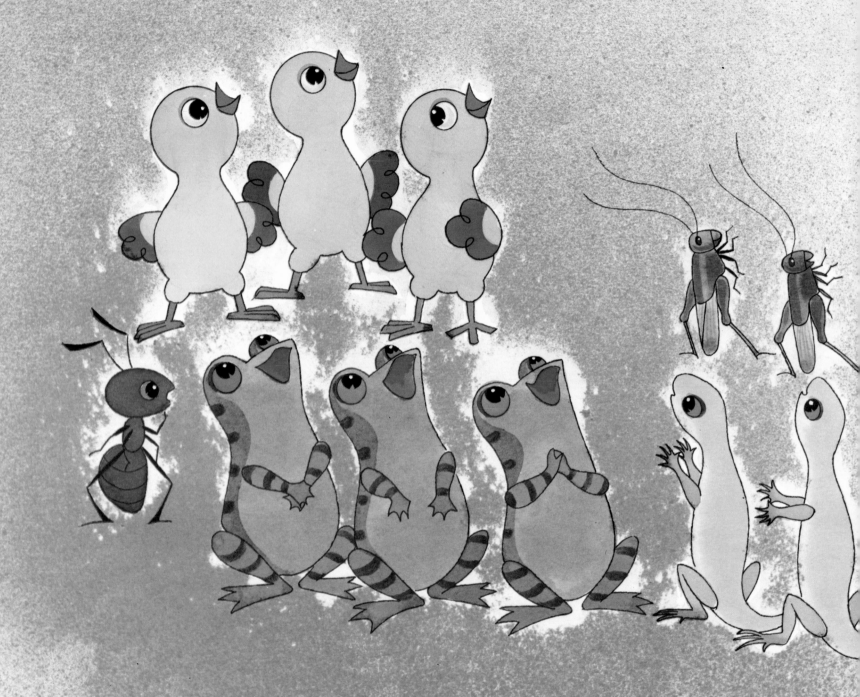

The baby frogs croaked at the wedding.
The baby birds sang their happy songs.
The grasshoppers danced and the crickets chirped.
The baby lizards clapped their hands.

After the party, Monty brought his bride home to the
little house in the hollow of the tree.

He took down his name and added Candy's name
 below his.
"This is our home," said Monty happily as he nailed
 the leaf outside their little home.